THIS BOOK BELONGS TO

First published in paperback in the United Kingdom by HarperCollins *Children's Books* in 2023

HarperCollins *Children's Books* is a division of HarperCollins*Publishers* Ltd
1 London Bridge Street, London SE1 9GF

www.harpercollins.co.uk

HarperCollins*Publishers*
Macken House, 39/40 Mayor Street Upper
Dublin 1, D01 C9W8, Ireland

1 3 5 7 9 10 8 6 4 2

Text by Alison Sage
Text copyright © HarperCollins*Publishers* Ltd 2023
Illustrations copyright © Sarah Gibb 2023

ISBN: 978–0–00–851409–9

Printed in the United Kingdom

HarperCollins *Children's Books*

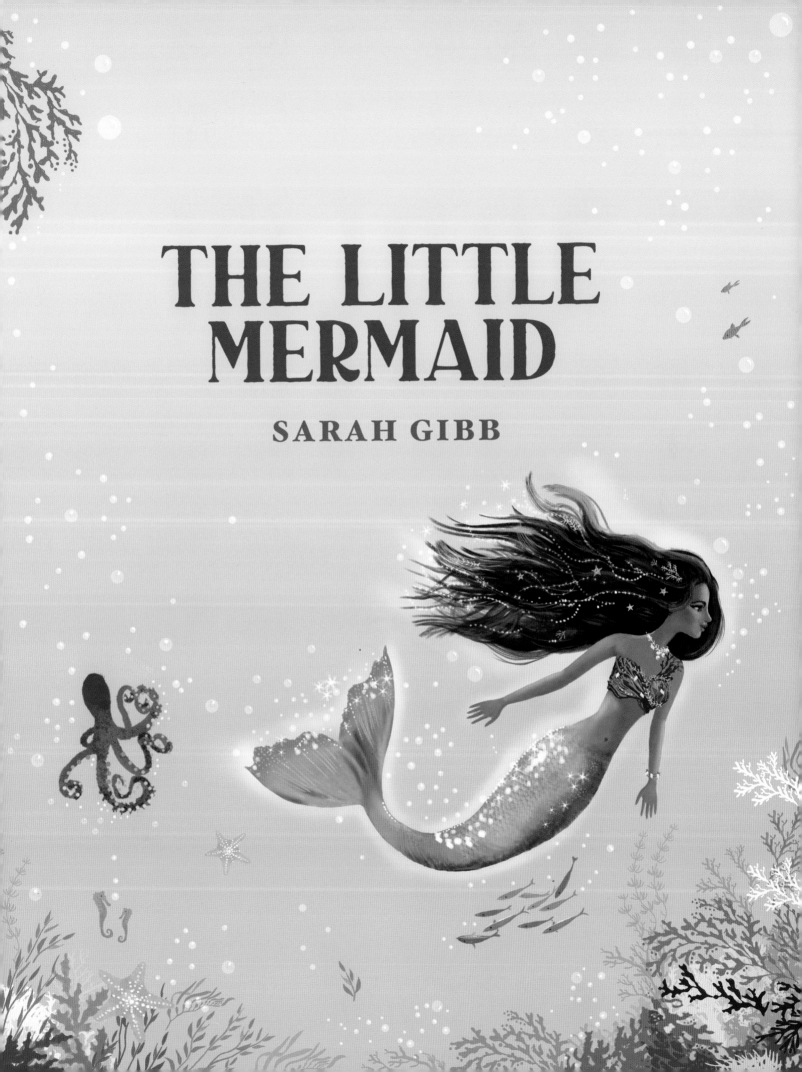

THE LITTLE MERMAID

SARAH GIBB

Far out at sea, the water is as blue as the petals of the loveliest cornflower and as clear as glass. There, the sea is very deep – so deep you cannot see the sandy floor. This is where the merpeople live as easily as anyone on land.

Many years ago, in the palace of the Sea King, lived the Little Mermaid. She was happy with her mermaid sisters and playing with her sea friends under the waves. She loved racing the little fish, playing hide-and-seek with the grumpy barnacles and singing to the tiny squid. All merpeople can sing – but the Little Mermaid had the most beautiful voice under the sea.

And yet, the Little Mermaid was not like the other mermaids.

The Little Mermaid was full of longing for . . . she wasn't quite sure what. She couldn't wait to be old enough to be allowed to see the world above water. Whatever was up there, it must be exciting and wonderful.

"I wish I didn't have to wait another whole year," she grumbled.

"There is danger for us merpeople up in the land of humans," said her mother wisely.

But the Little Mermaid wouldn't listen. "You think there is danger everywhere," she complained. "You are always warning me about the Sea Witch. She has never hurt me."

"That is because you have never been in her power," said her father, the Sea King. "Wait one more year."

The Little Mermaid swished her tail
and swam off. She stared through
the clear blue water of her world and
wished for the thousandth time
that she was allowed to swim
up to the humans above.

"Why can't I go?" she cried.
"Why? Why? Why?"

And then a wild and wonderful plan came into her head.

She would go by herself, up to the human world. She could slip through the waves and have a look. No one would know.

"Ooh. Don't do that!" sang the little fish.

"Don't be silly!" whined the seahorses. "Stay here with us."

But the Little Mermaid had made up her mind, and she began to swim upwards through the violet-blue water.

UP and UP and UP
she swam. Through
towers of ancient
coral . . .

past old shipwrecks
and forests of ferny
weed.

The light grew
stronger, and she
saw the silver roof
of the sea.
    She took a deep
breath and burst
through . . .

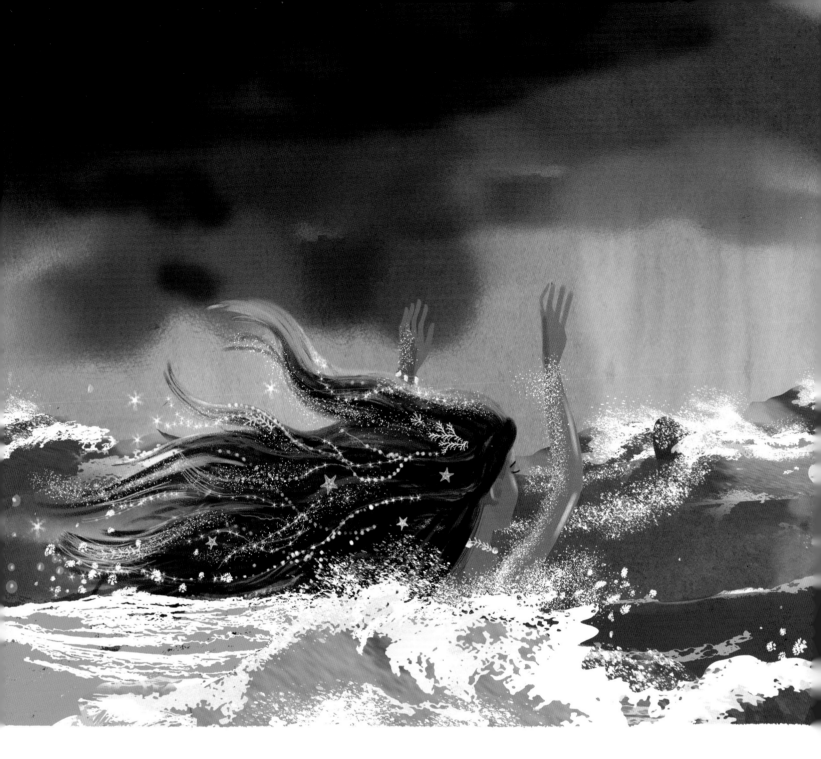

In front of her was a ship, lit up with lanterns, and she could hear the sounds of singing and happy voices. She knew it was forbidden, but the Little Mermaid swam closer to have a look.

"What a party!" she heard someone say. "The prince is always going to remember his birthday."

The music grew louder, and brightly dressed dancers flooded

out on to the deck. Leading them was a tall, smiling lad with dark hair – his face bright with excitement.

The Little Mermaid gasped. She longed to hear his name. She raised her arms out of the waves but no one saw her.

The wind was growing stronger, and the ship had started to rock up and down. A big storm was coming.

Lightning flashed overhead as the waves beat against the ship and the sailors struggled to keep it afloat.

The Little Mermaid watched amazed. *Why don't they dive into the sea?* she wondered.

The young prince stood for a moment while his friends huddled together. Turning to help the sailors, he slipped and tumbled into the waves.

And then the Little Mermaid remembered: *humans cannot breathe underwater*. He was going to drown. Quick as a flash, she dived and caught him as he whirled into the darkness. But he was taller than she was, and the Little Mermaid struggled to hold him as the waves dragged him away.

Slowly, very slowly, she brought the prince back to the surface and began the long swim towards the shore. His eyes were closed, and he was terribly pale, but the Little Mermaid would not give up. The storm was dying away as the Little Mermaid swam into shallow water. She cradled the prince in her arms, singing her most beautiful songs until the colour came back into his cheeks and his eyelids fluttered.

Just then, a shout rang out across the beach.

"I can see something floating! Quick – let's see what it is!" A crowd of villagers raced towards them.

The Little Mermaid was scared – she pushed the prince on to the sand and slipped under the water. Unseen, she watched as he sat up, confused, and opened his eyes. He was looking for her, but the villagers carried him away.

"If only I didn't have this tail," the Little Mermaid whispered to herself. "But now I will never see him again." And she swam sadly back to the Sea King's palace, where everyone was worried and angry.

That night, the Little Mermaid could not sleep. She could not stop thinking about the prince. At last, she got up and slipped out of the palace unseen. She was going to find the Sea Witch.

It was a dark and scary journey through caverns of tangled weed, and the Little Mermaid almost gave up many times. But there it was: the Sea Witch's home. And there was the Sea Witch herself.

"Please help me," begged the Little Mermaid. "I must walk on land like my dear prince, or he will never know that I saved his life."

"I will give you a pair of legs," hissed the Sea Witch. "Horrid things, legs. I don't know why you want them when you have a beautiful tail."

The Little Mermaid gasped. "Oh! Thank you—"

The Sea Witch interrupted. "I will make a bargain. You can have legs and go on land. But you must give me your voice. If your prince says he loves you before three days are over, my spell will be broken and you will have your voice back. But, if he doesn't . . . you will be in my power for ever."

The Little Mermaid didn't hesitate. "I will do whatever you want!" she cried.

The Sea Witch took the Little Mermaid's beautiful voice. It lay in her hand like a shining pearl.

"This is for me," she laughed, putting it in a seashell and tying it around her neck. "And this is for you!" She handed a glittering bottle to the Little Mermaid, who could now say not one word.

The Sea Witch disappeared, and the Little Mermaid found herself close to the beach where she had left the prince. Her fingers shaking, she took the stopper off the bottle and drank quickly. All of a sudden she had two shadowy legs under the water, and her tail had gone.

Bubbling with excitement, she ran on to the beach. It was such a strange feeling! Before long, she was walking through the palace gates.

The moment the Little Mermaid saw the prince she ached to talk to him. She opened her mouth, but not a sound came out.

The prince stared. "Can't you speak?" he asked. "I don't know why but somehow I feel as if I know you already!"

Oh, but you DO know me, thought the Little Mermaid. *There is no one in the world for me except you!*

And even though she couldn't talk, the two spent the rest of the day happily together, watching seals and seabirds and throwing pebbles into the warm sea. The next day passed in the same way.

The Little Mermaid would not have been so happy if she had known that the Sea Witch had sent out spies to the palace. And the spies carried a secret message for the prince's father, the king. "I'll soon put a stop to those two," hissed the Sea Witch as she waited for her evil plan to work.

On the third day the prince met the Little Mermaid again – but he was shocked and upset.

"My father had a message about the princess from the next country. And now he commands me to marry her," he told the Little Mermaid. "She is arriving tonight, and I must leave with her tomorrow. We have to say goodbye, my dear, quiet friend."

The Little Mermaid felt tears rush to her eyes. She couldn't bear to think of losing her prince for a second time.

She turned and fled through the royal gates, out of the palace and on to the beach where she had arrived – when her heart had been full of hope and happiness. But when the sun rose over the sea in the morning, she would be in the Sea Witch's power for ever.

In the palace, the prince raced from room to room, looking for the Little Mermaid. Why was she crying? Didn't she understand? They would still be friends. But he was a prince and he had to do what his father wanted.

Then he saw her alone on the beach. He ran towards her, and as he got closer he saw the waves rise up like mountains of blue glass and split open. Out stepped the Sea Witch, with her wand of sea snakes.

"You have lost your prince for ever, Little Mermaid," she laughed. "Why wait until tomorrow? Come with me now!"

The prince stared in horror. "Who are you?" he cried. "She doesn't belong to you!"

"The Little Mermaid is mine!" snarled the Sea Witch, and the sea foam flew like snowflakes into the air as she beat the water with her wand.

But the prince stood by the Little Mermaid's side. All of a sudden he knew he could not bear to lose her.

"I love her, and I want her to be with me always!"

As the prince spoke these words, the spell over the Little Mermaid was broken. The seashell around the witch's neck flew open and the Little Mermaid's beautiful voice tumbled out on to the sand.

Hurriedly she picked it up. At last, she could speak again.

"She is the Sea Witch!" cried the Little Mermaid. "And I am the girl who saved you from the sea. I gave her my voice so that I could walk on land and see you again."

The prince held the Little Mermaid's hand as she went on: "Go back to the sea caves where you belong, Sea Witch! Your power over me is finished."

The Sea Witch stormed away, and the sea boiled and foamed as she dived into the depths. She had lost. The Little Mermaid had found her prince.

It was a very happy day when the prince's family and the Little Mermaid's family agreed that their children should marry. The prince's father and mother held a big party, and the Sea King ordered that all storms were forbidden for two whole weeks while everyone celebrated. The Little Mermaid's sisters and all her sea

friends came to share her happiness, and the Sea King and Queen were delighted that their daughter had found such joy.

If the Little Mermaid was sad that she could no longer dive to the bottom of the sea she did not say so, because there were so many new things to discover on land.

Neither of their children were born with tails ... but they did love the sea and were never happier than when they were messing about in boats.

Some people said that the little prince and princess could swim like fish, but they have never found their way to the Sea King's palace. Maybe they will one day.